The Iron Claw

Paul Collins is the author of 140 books, including fantasy series *The Jelindel Chronicles*, The Quentaris Chronicles and *The World of Grrym* (in collaboration with Danny Willis).

Sean McMullen is the author of over a hundred fantasy and science fiction novels and stories, including *Souls in the Great Machine* and *Voyage of the Shadowmoon*. He was runner up for the Hugo Award in 2011.

Also by Paul Collins

The Jelindel Chronicles
The Quentaris Chronicles
The World of Grrym (with Danny Willis)
The Earthborn Wars
The Maximus Black Files

Also by Sean McMullen

Before the Storm
Changing Yesterday
The Ancient Hero
Souls in the Great Machine
Glass Dragons
Voyage of the Shadowmoon

THE IRON CLAW

Paul Collins and Sean McMullen

FORD ST

First published by Ford Street Publishing, an imprint of Hybrid
Publishers, PO Box 52, Ormond VIC 3204
Melbourne Victoria Australia

hybridpublishers.com.au

www.fordstreetpublishing.com

First published 2015

National Library of Australia Cataloguing-in-Publication entry
Creator: Collins, Paul, 1954– author.
Title: The iron claw / Paul Collins, Sean McMullen.

ISBN: xxx (paperback)

Series: Warlock's child: bk 3.

Target Audience: For primary school age.

Subjects: Fantasy fiction.

Other Creators/Contributors:
McMullen, Sean, 1948– author.

Dewey Number: A823.3

Printing and quality control in China by Tingleman Pty Ltd

To Jocelyn Pride – with many thanks for your support

GRONDAR
PANGVAI
MERK
TROPIC O
JAILING
QUANT
SECASTAR
ARCHIPELAGO
VARLIN
PALARA
GRENWELL
HALDAN
DRAVINIA

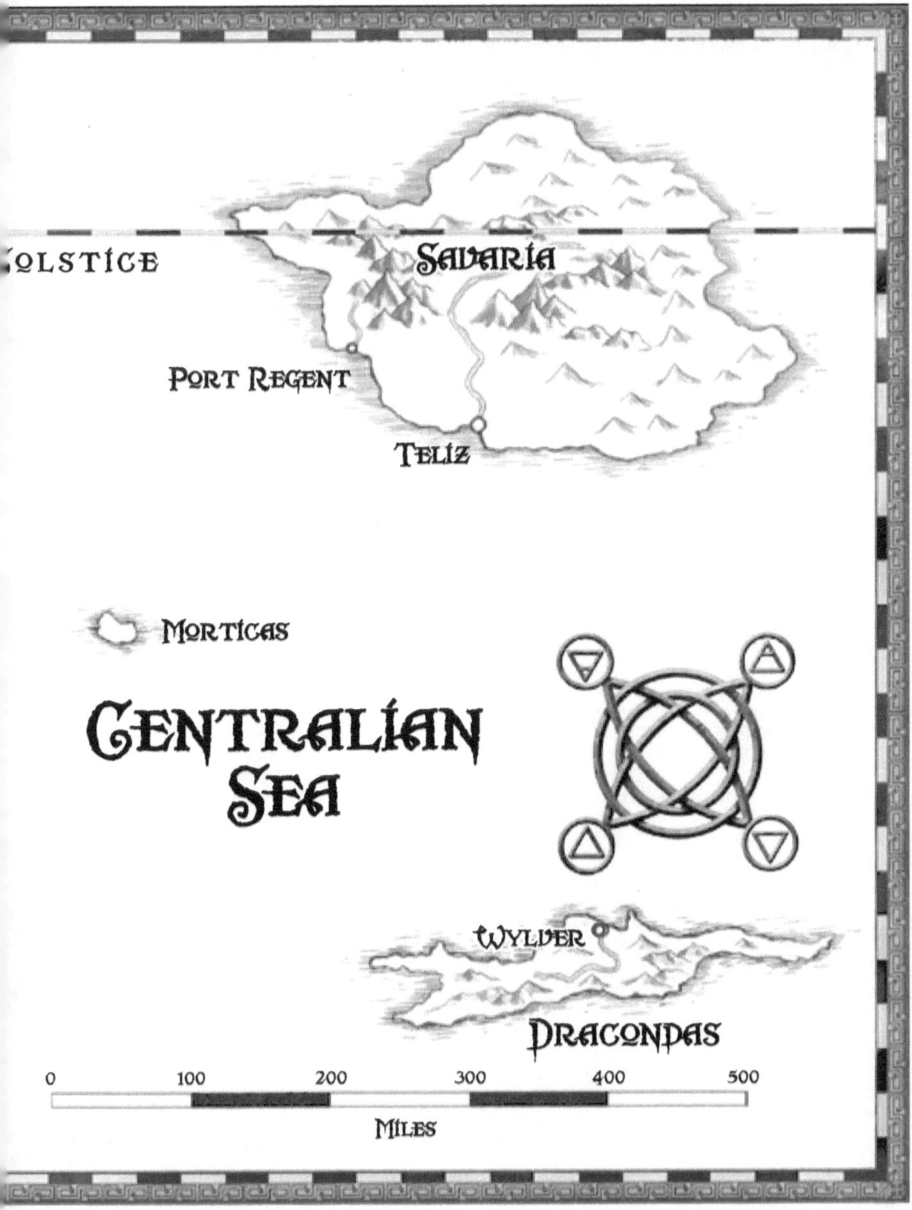

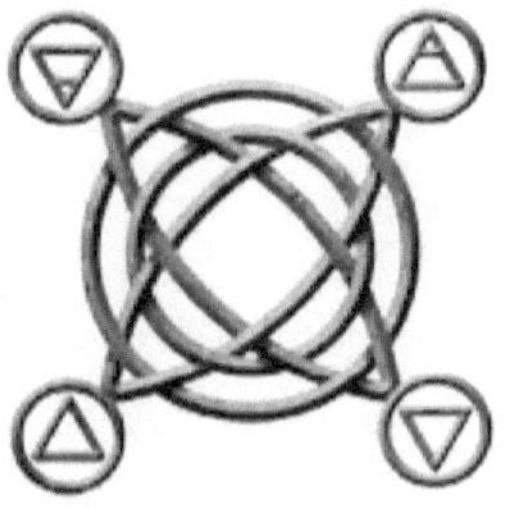

OLSTICE
SAVARIA
PORT REGENT
TELIZ
MORTICAS
CENTRALIAN SEA
WYLVER
DRACONDAS

0   100   200   300   400   500
MILES

DRAGONS

In the entire world there are few things that can strike fear into the heart of a king. The sight of his army retreating would be high on the list, and the royal taster clutching his stomach and collapsing would be even higher. At the very top, however, there could be nothing to rival three very angry dragons the size of warships towering over you and asking questions for which you have no answers.

Although King Lavarran II of Savaria was backed up by five thousand of the city militia and fifty of his shapecasters, he felt very exposed. He was standing on the open plain outside his capital, without the comforting walls of his palace to shield him from the forge-hot breath of the dragons – not that the palace walls would have stopped the dragons for very long.

The dragon Stormvaud had been in the city, tearing apart the old castle that was now being used as a prison, but now he was returning with evidence that humans were dabbling in magical arts that were forbidden to them. It would have been a very good time to run and hide, indeed a small group of militiamen had tried to do just this. One of the two dragons still standing before the king had breathed a thin streamer of green flame, and the six men and the cows that they were using as cover were reduced to piles of bones and charcoal in an oval patch of badly scorched pasture.

Nobody was going anywhere until the dragons were provided with an explanation about why forbidden magic was being practised in the city of Teliz.

The dragon Stormvaud circled the gathering once, then landed beside his companions with surprising grace for something of his size. Bending his head low, he lay two bodies on the ground before King Lavarran. The king looked down at them, and to his relief they looked quite human, in an ugly, over-muscled sort of way.

They were not dressed as anyone in his service.

Back among the members of the king's escort were two people wearing the armour that had been on the bodies only hours earlier. Both were from an enemy fleet that the king's forces had recently defeated.

Velza had not expected Latsar to take her by the hand, but she had not tried to pull away. After all, they were facing death by dragonfire within a few moments, and it was strangely comforting to think that she had experienced romance at least once in her life, if only for a few seconds.

The dragon Grimvaud looked down at the two bodies, then muttered some deep, rumbling words of power in a language that only his two companions understood. The two dead human guards shimmered, then re-formed as dead guard dogs.

'That's it, we're dead,' said Velza softly.

'*Explain this if you can,*' said the dragon Grimvaud. '*Shapeshifter magic, forbidden to humans since the war with the Dark Hands a thousand years ago. Forbidden under pain of death. These are creatures shapeshifted with earth, air, water and fire magic.*'

'Those are Crondarian troll hounds,' said the king at once. 'My guard dogs are mountain bullherders.'

'*Do not try to explain the unexplainable with technicalities,*' replied Grimvaud. '*Those creatures were in your city, and what is in your city is your responsibility.*'

It was now that Latsar suddenly strode forward, dragging Velza along with him.

'I can explain!' he shouted through the visor of his helmet.

The three dragons, the king, and everyone with a clear view turned to stare at them.

'*And who are you?*' demanded Grimvaud as the other two dragons lowered their heads to either side of Latsar.

'I am a secret agent of the king who stands before you,' replied Latsar. 'I have just returned from a mission to the enemy kingdom of Dravinia, and my codename is Longshadow.'

'*He tells the truth!*' said Videnveld, then she and Stormvaud raised their heads to confer with Grimvaud.

The outraged Velza pulled her hand from Latsar's grip.

'If I ever get a chance, I'll make you suffer for that!' she hissed.

'Beside me is a Dravinian secret agent known as the Iron Claw,' Latsar continued. 'She is working with me to expose a plot by her own father to put the ancient and forbidden magics back in the hands of humans.'

'I am?' whispered Velza.

Videnveld and Stormvaud again lowered their heads, this time to corner Velza.

'*Are you indeed a Dravinian known as the Iron Claw?*' Grimvaud asked.

'I am that person,' Velza replied, while thinking *even though it's just a silly name I'm called behind my back.*

'*She speaks the truth,*' reported Videnveld.

'*And are you in conflict with your father, who seeks to revive the forbidden magics?*' asked Grimvaud.

Velza tried to answer, but her father's spell made the words die before they left her mouth. She staggered about, clutching at her throat and trying to force the words out.

'*I sense dragon magic here,*' said Grimvaud, then he spoke some words aloud in the same incomprehensible language he had used while conferring with his companions.

Velza gave a great gasp, as if she had been choking and her throat had suddenly cleared.

'Yes!' she wheezed. 'Yes! Yes! Yes! Calbaras, my own father, has made himself my enemy. He cast a spell upon me, so that I could not speak of him.'

'*Also true,*' said Videnveld.

The two dragons raised their heads.

'*The warlock Calbaras does seem to have the forbidden dragon magic,*' said Stormvaud.

'*These shapeshifted bodies do indeed appear to be the work of a rogue human,*' said Grimvaud.

'*And humans are hunting for Calbaras, including his own daughter,*' said Videnveld.

'*That means the humans are allied with us in this matter,*' said Stormvaud. '*To flame this king and his army would be to do the very work of the rogue human warlock.*'

'*That would be unthinkable,*' said Videnveld.

Grimvaud looked down at the king.

'*I am satisfied that you are acting in good faith,*' he declared, '*and that you and your army do not deserve annihilation. Find this warlock Calbaras, and bring me proof that it is he that has dabbled in dark and forbidden arts.'*

'It will be done, we are allies in this matter,' replied King Lavarran.

One after the other the three dragons took to the air, and again the downdraft from their wings blew many of the guardsmen and their horses off their feet. After picking himself up, the king walked over to Latsar and Velza.

'Longshadow, welcome home,' he said as the pair knelt before him. 'Oh get up, for goodness sake! You just saved my life, *I* should be kneeling to *you*.'

'Your Majesty, permit me to introduce the Iron Claw,' said Latsar, with an elaborate gesture to Velza.

Velza bowed, and was extremely grateful that the visor of her helmet hid her blushing cheeks.

'So, you are a Dravinian spy, and a lady as well,' said the king. 'How wonderful. I thought only men had a chance to be dashing and romantic.'

'I'm afraid it's mainly hard work and danger, your Majesty,' Velza replied.

'Well, for now the danger has passed. Come

along, let us return to the city and clean up at the palace, then I can hear what you have to say over dinner. I'm very curious to see what you look like without the helmet.'

DANTAR

Under the city, deep within its sewers, Velza's brother would have been safe from an attack by the three dragons. Nevertheless, he was still in a great deal of danger.

'I've never seen so many rats in one place,' said Dantar as he and Marko stood together in the reeking gloom.

'Just don't step on them,' said Marko.

'Could be your last mistake,' said a rat perched on a pipe emptying slime into the main sewer.

'Do I have the honour of addressing the rat king?' asked Marko.

'Rats have kings?' said Dantar.

'I am just a prince,' explained the rat. 'Merikus is my name.'

Marko went down on one knee.

'Kneel!' he hissed.

'Kneel?' exclaimed Dantar. 'We're in a sewer,

ankle deep in everything that goes down the privy. Besides, he's a rat.'

'He's a rat with a title and an army! Now kneel!'

Dantar knelt in the cold, clinging sludge. He had heard about rat princes, but he thought they did not exist outside of children's stories.

'What are you doing in my tunnels, humans?' demanded Merikus. 'I heard the stupid one say that he was a hunter of rats. Might you two be down here to hunt us?'

Merikus spoke in a squeaky, chittery voice, and another rat seemed to be translating for the benefit of his subjects. There was a lot of agitated chittering when he got to the part about hunting rats.

'We are lost, we only seek guidance so that we may leave,' said Marko.

'How could anyone be so stupid as to get lost down here?' replied Merikus. 'Anyway, why should I help you? Why don't I just have you bitten to death for being rat hunters?'

'Because helping us would increase your status, Prince Merikus. Your followers have seen humans kneeling before you. That makes you look important. If you show us how to leave, we shall owe you a big favour. Can you imagine that? Two humans in debt to a rat?'

'No rat would care,' replied Merikus. 'We already have all the rubbish we could ever eat from you humans.'

'Then be a hero,' said Dantar, suddenly remembering how much flattery went on in the royal courts of humans. 'You have two human rat hunters cornered in your principality. If you were to just force us to leave without killing any of your subjects, think of how impressed your subjects would be.'

'Why would that make me a hero?'

'Because in the battle, we would kill a lot of rats before you could kill us.'

'Ha!' said the rat, eying Dantar. 'For someone so stupid you have clever ideas.'

'Will you help us?' asked Marko.

'Saving rat lives is good, but I would also be letting you go. That will not look good to my subjects. What are you offering as payment?'

'Payment?' snorted Dantar. 'For a rat?'

'Hand something over or my subjects might decide they want someone else as a prince.'

Marko reached down into his left boot and withdrew a golden ring set with a beautiful green stone.

'Family heirloom,' said Marko. 'Old rolled gold.'

Merikus took the ring in his tiny hands and like a jeweller eyed it closely. After several long moments, the rat looked up.

'Some of the gold seems to have rolled off,' he said.

'So? It's old,' said Marko.

'And the green stone doesn't shine like an emerald.'

'What do sewer rats know about emeralds?'

'You'd be surprised what gets tossed down the privies when human wives are arguing with human husbands.'

'I'll tie it around your head with a strip of cloth and it can be your crown.'

'A crown! I like that. What do you think, my subjects?'

The translator rat translated. Hundreds of little voices chittered and squeaked with excitement. The rats definitely approved. Dantar tore part of a trouser cuff away and used it to improvise a headband for the rat.

'I crown thee Prince Merikus the First of the Undercity,' said Marko as he tied the ring on the rat's head.

The squeals of excitement went on for a very long time.

'You, stupid one!' said Merikus. 'I must have a steed to ride, so that everyone will know my status.'

'I've never heard of a horse in a sewer,' said Dantar.

'Oh, that's all right, I can ride on your head.'

Breath hissed between Dantar's teeth, but Marko clamped a filthy hand over his mouth.

'It's just until we get out of here!' said Marko hurriedly. Then he placed Merikus on Dantar's head.

'I do believe that I'm now in a position to help,' said Merikus.

'We must make our way to the docks,' said Marko.

'Easy, when there's a rat to guide you. Lots of good pickings at the docks, and a lot of relatives visiting on the ships. I know all the right holes to crawl through.'

'Big enough for a human to squeeze through?' asked Dantar.

'Could be a tight squeeze, but yes.'

'Do we have a contract?' asked Marko. 'Do you swear by earth magic that you will carry out your promise to get us safely out of this place?'

'Do I really have to?'

'You really do.'

'Very well, then. I swear.'

'Great,' said Marko. 'Now lead on.'

'You, steed, walk forward for thirty paces, then turn left into the next branch tunnel,' said Merikus to Dantar.

Dantar set off, with Marko following behind.

'We must be crazy,' muttered Dantar, once they were away from the other rats. 'Trusting a *rat* to get us out of here! Why do you think someone invented the term "ratting out your friends"?'

Marko sighed. 'According to custom, we've entered into a contract bound by earth magic, Dantar. Merikus *cannot* break it, unless *we* betray him.'

'But neither of us is an earth shapecaster.'

'A contract entered underground and sworn by earth magic is binding. We can tell the next earth shapecaster that we meet if we are betrayed, and he can do horrible things to Merikus.'

'We won't *be* around to complain!' Dantar said, exasperated.

'No need to fret,' said Merikus. 'I'm a rat of honour.'

'I still don't like it,' muttered Dantar.

'Turn here,' said Merikus. 'Left again.'

Although the sewers were dark, a slimy phosphorescent fungus glowed from the walls here and there. It reeked like rotting flesh, and dripped on them as they passed. Where the drips fell, their clothing glowed.

'How much farther?' Dantar gasped, fighting back another urge to be sick.

'We're here,' said Merikus.

They'd stopped where some bricks had crumbled and fallen from the roof of the sewer tunnel. Above their heads Dantar could see only darkness.

'You first,' said Marko.

He made a stirrup with his hands and boosted Dantar up through the hole. He was tall enough to grasp the edge and pull himself up. Then, by the light from the fungal drips on their own clothing, they stood and surveyed the chamber. It was dry, and the air was a little fresher than down in the sewer, yet there was still a suggestion of rotting flesh. They seemed to now be in a maze of tunnels made of old brick, and rooms branched out continually from the main tunnel as they walked.

'What is this place?' asked Dantar.

'The catacombs,' said Merikus, still on top of his head.

'That's nice,' Dantar said. 'From the sewers of the city to the city of the dead!'

'You might want to keep your voice down, too,' added Merikus.

'Why?'

'Because there are *things* here.'

Dantar felt the hairs on the back of his neck stand up. *Things?* 'What happens if we meet any . . . things?' he asked.

Merikus snorted. 'Then you'll have to use your magic, won't you, boy?'

'Well, that could be a problem, because *I don't have any magic*!'

'Keep your voice down,' said Marko, 'and move a little faster, before we're noticed.'

Dantar had the feeling that Merikus was nervous too. That worried him. An hour later, they'd stumbled, crawled and jogged through nearly three miles of the labyrinth of burial chambers.

'Nearly at the docks,' said Merikus. 'Don't know why you want to go there, though. The Dravinian soldiers burned most of the ships and stole the rest.'

'What?' gasped Dantar and Marko together.

'There are no ships. None that are above water, anyway.'

Dantar snatched Merikus off his head, held him very firmly in one hand and glared at him.

'Listen, rat, why would we want to get to the docks, except to escape on a ship?' he snarled.

'There's all sorts of scraps to be stolen —'

'I think he meant why would we *humans* want to go there, except to get passage somewhere — anywhere — on a ship,' said Marko.

'I think you're being very unreasonable,' said Merikus. 'It was an honest mistake.'

'Get us to the surface, now!' snapped Dantar.

'Somewhere where there's a bath, soap and clean clothes.'

'I'll have to think about that,' replied Merikus. 'We rats don't wear clothes or have baths – Wait! Stop. Stop here.'

They stopped at the entrance to a large arched chamber. The faint, fungoid glow from their clothing did not reach far enough to light up all the corners. Dantar opened his hand, and Merikus sat up on his palm, sniffing the air and twitching his whiskers.

'Don't like it,' he muttered.

'Don't like what?' asked Dantar.

'Wasn't talking to *you*,' snapped Merikus.

'You're only pretending that there's danger so I won't strangle you.'

'Something very odd down here,' squeaked Merikus. 'Never smelt anything like it, except . . .' He eyed Dantar.

'Yes?'

'Smells a bit like *you*.'

'Me?' exclaimed Dantar. 'I don't *smell*.'

'All humans smell. Actually, they stink. You especially.'

'Well, take us to a bathhouse,' said Dantar as

he took one step out into the huge chamber.

He stopped, his second step suspended in mid-stride. Shrill, cackling laughter echoed through the great, dim chamber. It was not the laughter of someone enjoying a good joke; it was more like that of a monster that had just cornered its victim.

VELZA

ost of the militiamen and constables had to walk back from the meeting with the dragons, but the king and his guards and shapecasters were mounted. Velza and Latsar shared a horse provided by a junior shapecaster who was now walking.

'You are not forgiven,' said Velza as they rode. 'You tricked me, you lied to me —'

'I never lied to you, I just didn't tell the whole truth,' retorted Latsar.

'Well, what now? Do I get put in chains and locked in a dungeon?'

'I think both of us will be put in baths, given clean clothes and fed dinner — probably with the king.'

'Just for fooling a dragon?'

'No, for saving the king, five thousand of his men, and probably the entire city from being flamed down to the bedrock. You and I are heroes, try to remember that.'

'So what do I say when the king talks to me? He thinks I'm the Iron Claw, a secret agent.'

'So? That's what the other officers called you behind your back aboard the *Invincible*.'

'I suppose you did too.'

'It's a great name.'

'And I'm not a secret agent.'

'Yes you are. You're a Dravinian officer, doing things secretly in a Savarian city. I do admit that nobody appointed you, but who else needs to know that?'

'If you have all the answers, tell me what I should say to the king.'

'Tell him that your father is up to something bad, and that we need the freedom of the city to hunt him down.'

'Why should he listen to us?'

'See those dragons up there, circling the city?'

'Yes.'

'The king wants them to go away. He also thinks that you might be able to help.'

The ladies in waiting who were assigned to Velza were surprised when she took off her armour and revealed herself to be a girl. When she took off her tunic they had an even bigger surprise.

'You have muscles!' exclaimed Lady Marial. 'What girl has muscles?'

'I'm a shapecaster soldier,' replied Velza. 'The muscles help when I need to kill people.'

'But ladies should have champions to do that sort of thing.'

'Sorry, I like to catch and kill my own.'

'Ladies should at least use poison if they have to kill,' said Lady Dienair.

'Poison is no use on the battlefield, because the enemy is not eating dinner. Speaking of fighting, I twisted my ankle in the fighting yesterday. Can you find a physician to bind it up properly after I have my bath?'

Velza was again dressed as a mercenary when she was escorted into the king's presence. Latsar, also dressed as a mercenary, was already there. *They are on suspiciously familiar terms,* thought Velza, as she approached a table covered with food and jugs of wine. Two overweight hunting hounds looked up at her, decided that she was no threat, and turned their attention back to the table.

'Your limp has almost vanished,' said Lavarran as Velza took her seat.

'Your physician was very skilled, your Majesty, thank you,' she replied.

'You stride like a soldier, that's good. Most women dressed up as men still move like ladies and so betray themselves.'

'I can be a lady if I have to.'

'Just the sort of talent a spy needs – but you are not eating. Please, take whatever you fancy.'

Lavarran and Latsar chatted while the famished Velza ate five chicken legs and a bowl of salad, then drank some watered ale.

'You eat plain fare,' said Lavarran.

'Assassins expect nobles to eat the best, so they poison the best.'

'Quite so, that's why my hounds get what the royal kitchen prepares for me. The servants think that the hounds get what you and I eat.'

'Wise of you, your Majesty.'

'I'm young for a king, don't you think?'

'Reigning well is more important than a

monarch's age, your Majesty,' said Velza.

'Well put. I like to think I am a good ruler. My oldest brother had Father murdered because he was living too long. He was impatient to be King, you see. Then my sister poisoned him on the night of the coronation. She ruled as Regent for a while, because I was still too young to be crowned. When I turned fourteen, and was old enough to take the throne, she decided that she liked being Regent, so she tried to poison me as well.'

'You're still alive,' observed Velza.

'I suspected that someone had bad intentions for me, so I added a harmless philter to my own orange juice. Drink it, and it was as safe as drinking rainwater from the sky. Add a poison like spiderbane to it, and it bubbles up as if a red-hot horseshoe were dropped in. My sister was smiling as she bent over the jug and added the spiderbane powder from her trick ring. When the mixture frothed up, some got into her mouth.'

'And she poisoned herself,' added Latsar.

'You are in my position, Lady Velza,' said Lavarran. 'Just because someone is family, they must still prove themselves worthy of trust. That was true of my older brother and my sister, and it is true of your father.'

'Your father is dabbling in the four magics,' said Latsar. 'If he were to put them back together, he would become a Dark Hand, a warlock as powerful as a dragon. He has been to Teliz before, and he persuaded King Lavarran that the Dravinians were plotting to do precisely that. He then returned and convinced the Dravinian emperor that the Savarians were doing the same thing.'

'That makes no sense!' exclaimed Velza. 'Nobody would gain anything.'

'Calbaras would,' said Lavarran. 'The finest shapecasters on the Centralian Sea would be sent into the fighting, and would die. Then who would there be to stop Calbaras?'

'The dragons, of course,' said Velza.

'We think he has some scheme to defeat the dragons as well,' said Latsar.

'But *I* was one of the shapecasters on the fleet,' said Velza.

'Remember, even family must prove themselves worthy of trust,' replied Lavarran. 'Latsar and I learned that at a very early age.'

'Latsar's your brother?' cried Velza, rising to her feet and waving a chicken leg at the young officer.

Latsar put a hand over his eyes. Lavarran drummed his fingers on the table. Several guards rushed into the dining chamber, but Lavarran waved them out again.

'I thought you knew,' said the king once Velza had sat down again.

'No!' exclaimed Velza, who was now recalling the whole of her time with Latsar. 'He swore to serve loyally in my squad, he fought the dragon beside me, then he got me demoted, yet he saved me from my own father . . . But all the while he was a cunning, devious enemy spy. Just whose side is he on?'

'Spies do have to be secretive,' said Lavarran.

'He even held my hand!'

'Did he really? And here was I thinking that young Lady Elvina had won his heart – and I gather that not a few Dravinian ladies fancied him as well.'

'Well I am one Dravinian lady who is not in the queue,' said Velza.

'Could we return to discussing your father?' said Latsar. 'After all, he is in this city, and has truly evil intentions.'

'I'd rather rot in a dungeon as an enemy spy than help you. Why don't you ask the king for a medal for exposing such a dangerous person as me, the Iron Claw?'

'Consider that the king is sitting in front of you,' warned Latsar.

'My apologies,' said Velza.

'No offence taken,' said Lavarran.

'Getting back to your father,' began Latsar.

'If you're such a good spy, then you find him!' snapped Velza.

'I'm afraid I must insist that you two cooperate,' said Lavarran. 'Of all the people loyal to me in the city, you two know Calbaras best. Please, for the sake of stopping this silly war with your own people and saving us all from the dragons, just find this rogue warlock and hand him over to my guards.'

Velza pushed back from the table and frowned in thought for a few moments.

'My brother Dantar, the son of the Warlock Calbaras, is somewhere in the city. Father was doing something odd with Dantar. At first I thought that it was just to help him develop shapecasting powers, but now I am not so sure. Find Dantar and eventually Calbaras will come for him.'

'But if Dantar is still alive he will be in hiding too,' said Latsar. 'He is an enemy officer, you know.'

'Well, you're the spy prince. *You* find him.'

'Gentlefolk, please, you do need to work together,' said Lavarran, who then held up his hand and snapped his fingers.

A servant entered with a small box on a red cushion with gold tassels. The young king took the box, but did not open it until the servant had left.

'Now then, Lady Velza, you really are an enemy spy, even though your intentions seem far from evil. I cannot grant you rewards or titles without risking discontent among my subjects, but I would like to give you this little token of my appreciation.'

'Your Majesty, thank you,' said Velza, taking the box from him and opening it.

Within was a ring with the Savarian royal crest,

a half-Moonlet on a half-Moon. It fitted perfectly on the little finger of Velza's left hand.

'Just a small trifle that I had my jeweller run up while you bathed and ate. The physician who attended you also measured your finger for the fit. Now press the Moonlet shape.'

Velza did so, then gasped with surprise as a little metal claw sprang free. It clicked back into place when she pressed it from behind.

'An iron claw for the Iron Claw,' said Lavarran. 'It may even be useful if you are ever in need of a small but wickedly sharp blade. Thank you for saving my life and my city, Lady Velza.'

DRAGONS

High above the city, in the light of early evening, the three dragons circled together, seeking other dragons. Apart from themselves there were no others nearby.

'*I sensed a chick, just as we arrived, then it vanished,*' said Grimvaud.

'*I did too,*' said Videnveld. '*It was fleeting, so very fleeting.*'

'*Could it have died?*' asked Stormvaud.

'*No, we would have sensed the flash of its spirit ending,*' said Videnveld.

'*Then where is it?*'

'*Hiding.*'

'*From us?*'

'*Perhaps.*'

'*Why?*'

'*It is very small. Our size may frighten it.*'

'*That means it has been raised away from other dragons,*' said Grimvaud. '*How can this be? We know of every egg laid.*'

'*Not quite,*' said Stormvaud. '*My sister Fernveld vanished without trace fifteen years ago. She may have laid an egg that we have not tallied.*'

'*Then the chick may be the key to her fate. Who was her mate?*'

'*Alas, Dravaud,*' said Stormvaud, glancing to the very large crater in the side of a distant mountain, then flattening his crest in sorrow.

'*Long may his spirit soar upon the winds,*' responded Grimvaud.

'*One of us should fly to Dracondas and tell the others what has happened here,*' said Stormvaud. '*I shall do so now.*'

Down in the city there was cautious rejoicing that one of the dragons had left. Because the king had been talking to the dragons, it was assumed that he had something to do with the dragon leaving. Loyal toasts were drunk in taverns, and a small crowd gathered at the palace gates to cheer.

DANTAR

Deep underground, Dantar was still alive, but not certain about how much longer he would stay that way.

'Danthar,' came a halting voice. 'Come tho me . . .'

Dantar shot a look at Marko, but the youth was just as frightened, if not more so. Nothing down here was to be trusted apart from himself and possibly Marko, so whoever or whatever knew his name was sure to have bad intentions.

'Do noth fear me . . .' the voice called again.

'Don't speak to strange voices!' said Marko, grabbing Dantar's arm.

The pair broke into a run, hurrying back the way they'd come, then swerved into the next tunnel mouth. From somewhere behind came more eerie laughter. Panting, they pounded down a sloping tunnel. Dantar's skin was still prickling with fear when he saw an intersection ahead.

'Something bad, stop, stop, stop!' cried Merikus, who was still clutched in Dantar's hand. The youths tried to stop, skidded together, then fell sliding across the intersection with the other tunnel. A tongue of green flame blasted above them. Its heat was so intense that they would have been roasted alive from the waist up if they had been on their feet. Looking back, Dantar saw clumps of tree roots from the city above that were on fire.

'Dantar . . .'

'Get up, run straight ahead, then turn right,' said Merikus.

Dantar and Marko did as ordered.

'You cannot flee . . .' said the voice, but it was growing fainter now.

What seemed like hours later, but was probably only minutes, Dantar and the rat crouched at the mouth of a tunnel that overhung a large crypt. Old bones and skulls were piled everywhere, and beyond the piles was a wide, dark pool of foul water.

Marko was some way behind, resting. The

continual chase through the tunnels, along with the fall into the sea and battering on the rocks, had taken a heavy toll on him.

'We have to cross *that*?' said Dantar, pointing to the pool and holding Merikus up with his other hand.

'That's right,' Merikus replied. 'You can swim, fly or take a boat.'

'There's a boat?'

'No, but –'

'Oh, give it a rest! I can't swim, and Marko is in no condition to swim through that muck, especially towing you and me.'

Just then he heard soft footsteps, and he pushed the hair out of his eyes as he turned.

'Marko, I told you to get some rest while I checked for danger –' he began, then stopped.

It wasn't Marko. Dantar stood up slowly, fairly sure that he was facing danger but not sure about what that danger could do to him. On the palm of his hand, Merikus's little head was swivelling back and forth, his jaw hanging open. The boy facing them was Dantar's identical twin.

'Who are you?' asked Dantar. 'And don't bother saying that you're me because I'm the one person who definitely knows the truth there.'

'I am Avantar. Keep thalking, I need tho hear more of your voith tho – so – I can improve my speech.'

Dantar took a step backwards, vaguely aware he was on the brink of a pit. Below him was a ten-foot drop to a pile of bones. He swallowed.

'What do you want?'

'I want tho – to – be you, and I am getting better at it all the time.'

VELZA

Nobody expected a girl to wear an eye patch, so by wearing a cloth wound around her head and covering one eye, Velza both disguised her face and looked like she was a youth. Thus she could dress like a man, without causing comment in a city where women went about in elaborate, flowing robes.

'Don't think I'm impressed just because you're a prince and heir to the throne,' she muttered to Latsar as they walked through the palace, dressed as Lyridian mercenaries.

'As soon as he's married and has a child, I'll no longer be heir.'

'Just as well. King of Spies! Just imagine how much the other kingdoms would trust Savaria.'

'Anyway, I don't want to be King. I prefer girls to like me for being charming, not for my title.'

'This girl doesn't like you for either!'

'Remember that you're not meant to be a girl.'

'Well, try to remember that yourself.'

'So where do we look for your father?' Latsar asked.

'Stop calling him my father! I'm ashamed to be of his bloodline.'

'Well, where do we look for the warlock Calbaras?'

'We question the entire surviving garrison from the prison castle.'

'They won't talk.'

'No, but they can be persuaded to give themselves away. I have been in the Dravinian royal court since I was twelve, I know how to make people give themselves away without realising it. But first, I want to look at those two dead hounds.'

The bodies of the hounds were being kept in the palace dungeons. Once they had been large, powerful dogs that inspired fear, but now they were just cold stiff corpses that bore the marks of the dragon Stormvaud's teeth.

'What were they like in life?' asked Velza. 'I mean, when they were shapeshifted into people?'

'Diligent and strong, but not very bright,' said Latsar. 'They showed unquestioning loyalty without much initiative.'

'How did you defeat them?'

'I walked straight up to the door waving a scroll with the royal seal in my hand and said it was an important message from the king. As the one on the left turned to open the door I stabbed the one on the right with a dagger, which was concealed in the scroll. In the split second it took for the other to turn back I drew the dagger at my belt and stabbed him in the throat, just under the chin.'

'Wait a moment, when did you get a chance to have your brother put his seal on a scroll?'

Latsar performed an elaborate flourish, like a children's conjuror, then held out his hand to display a ring of office on his palm.

'I didn't. I stole his ring last year to annoy him, and had a couple of copies made before I gave it back. Would you like one?'

Velza picked up the ring and peered at it closely.

'Best not to wear it,' said Latsar. 'Not unless you somehow become queen.'

Velza struggled with her conscience for a moment, then dropped the ring into her purse.

'Getting back to these dogs,' she said, 'they had human shape, could speak, and probably thought that they were humans. What does that tell us?'

'That your father is good at his job?'

'It tells us that he's *impossibly* good at his job. Humans can't do this sort of magic. One needs command of the fire of life, the earth of bodies, the water of blood and the air of breath. Only dragons can do all four magics, so he must have used a dragon to do the shapecasting.'

'The other dragons would be a bit annoyed about that.'

'Annoyed? They would have it executed.'

'So now what?'

'I think . . . we make an announcement that Dantar has been found, and is being held in a palace tower. Calbaras will be sure to come for him.'

'But Dantar is your brother, the *big disappointment* Dantar, the *family disgrace* Dantar. He has no magic, he's no use to anyone.'

'Don't jump to conclusions. Last year Father

was summoned to the island of Dracondas, to be questioned by the dragons. They asked him if he had forbidden knowledge, and he said no. They can tell when humans are lying, yet they were satisfied with his answers. Suppose, just suppose, he put Dantar into a trance and made him read forbidden books. Dantar would be like a living book, a forbidden living book.'

'But you said Calbaras tried to kill Dantar.'

'What would you do if a dragon was closing in and you had a forbidden book on your ship?'

Latsar nodded, and for once he was not smiling. 'Toss it overboard. And here was I thinking that only princes had homicidal families.'

'Quite by accident, Dantar survived,' Velza said. 'He is still worth more to Calbaras than the crown jewels of Dravinia's emperor, so the warlock will want his child back. Will your brother do as I ask?'

'Probably, but if not I can put his seal of approval on your plan,' said Latsar, tossing another forged royal ring of office in the air and catching it.

DANTAR

Dantar had always had doubts about who he really was. His mother was in fact his stepmother, and while she was never cruel and did not bully him, she was a powerful sorceress and treated him more like a disappointing experiment than a child. Perhaps he really did have a twin brother, separated from him at birth. Both boys reached up and pushed the hair from their eyes at the same time. *Identical gestures.* Dantar jerked his hand back. So did Avantar. It was like watching himself in a mirror!

'I'm dreaming,' he said. 'Maybe I hit my head . . .'

'I didn't hit mine,' said Merikus, 'and *I'm* seeing you talking to you.'

'Interesting friends you have, Dantar,' said Avantar.

'We aren't friends!' Dantar and Merikus said together.

Avantar smiled – then sprang. He cannoned into Dantar, and both boys plummeted backwards into a pit, arms and legs flailing. They landed on a pile of bones that were centuries old, and had long ago been removed from the crypts to make way for the newly dead.

Avantar seized Dantar's arm, but Dantar snatched up a leg bone and smashed it down on Avantar's wrist. Avantar cried out and let go, but as Dantar clambered back up the pile of bones a hand snagged his leg. He kicked backwards with his other leg, and heard a grunt of pain.

Dantar had just reached the top of the pile of bones and was scrabbling for the ledge above when a body tumbled over the edge and landed on top of him. Again he went tumbling down the pile of bones.

Avantar seized him.

'Dantar, what is this?' called Marko's voice in the gloom. 'There's two of you.'

'I'm the real one!' shouted Dantar and Avantar together as they struggled.

Dantar punched Avantar in the stomach, but

the other boy was much stronger and pinned his arms. Avantar opened his mouth wide.

Dantar screamed in terror. At the back of Avantar's throat was a vortex of green flame.

A torrent of raging green fire poured out over Dantar's face . . . yet to Dantar it was no worse than being shouted at by someone with bad breath.

Avantar blinked with surprise, his mouth still open.

Remembering what he had learned during fights with other cabin boys aboard the warship *Invincible*, Dantar head-butted Avantar on the nose.

Avantar fell backwards into the dark pool at the edge of the pile of bones and sank out of sight.

'What was that thing?' Dantar gasped.

'While we're asking embarrassing questions, what are you?' asked Marko. 'Your twin had dragon's breath, yet you took the full blast in your face without so much as a singed eyebrow.'

'Yeah, and look what it did to the bones behind you,' said Merikus from the top of one of the skulls.

Dantar turned. The bones at the top of the pile had been turned to white dust, and the bricks of the wall behind them were melted into a sort of glaze.

Marko snatched Merikus off the skull.

'It's strange, you know, but Dantar tells me that some baby dragon keeps arriving just in time to save his life,' he said. 'It's a shapeshifting dragon, and it's been a seagull, a cat, and maybe even a bat.'

'And now it's a dirty little rat,' added Dantar.

'I may be dirty, little, and a rat, but I'm not a dirty little rat,' said Merikus, squirming in Marko's grip. 'I'm not a were-dragon, either.'

'And I'm the Emperor of Dravinia,' said Marko.

'Well, thanks for casting that fire shield and saving me,' said Dantar.

'I'm just a rat, I didn't do it,' insisted Merikus.

'Let's discuss this later,' said Dantar, waving at the pool of foul, dark water. 'I can't swim. Can you tow us, Marko?'

'Not without a long sleep and a good meal. I'm so sore and tired I can hardly crawl.'

'Why not paddle across?' squeaked Merikus.

'You said there was no boat,' said Dantar.

'There's coffins, dumb human! The deathwalkers use them to paddle across the pool with the bones.'

'Deathwalkers?' echoed Dantar anxiously.

'Just the men who carry the bodies and bones about in the catacombs,' said Marko. 'They make the dead seem to walk, so they're called deathwalkers. They're not very dangerous.'

'No more than anyone else,' added Merikus. 'Come along, over to the left. The deathwalkers usually leave a few coffins there.'

Taking the coffin of what must have once been a particularly large man, Dantar and Marko paddled out across the pool. The paddles were human shoulder blades tied to leg bones, but they worked surprisingly well. On the other side of the pool were stone steps, and the air seemed a little fresher. Marko carried Merikus because Dantar refused to, and after three hundred steps they came to another tunnel. This one was wider, and lined with freshly painted wooden covers, with words written on most of them.

They now stopped to rest. Dantar's legs were wobbly after the climb, and Marko could hardly crawl. As they massaged their leg muscles, Dantar reminded himself that he also had every right to feel battered and exhausted. After surviving the leap off the castle's battlements and the pounding waves on the rocks below, he had been running, hiding or fighting for a full day. He dearly wanted to sleep.

'"Feldinius Aclar",' Marko said, reading the words on a nearby panel by the light glowing from the fungal fluids on his clothing. '"When I die, don't bury me deep, leave one hand free, to fleece the sheep"'. This may be the very man we need.'

'Why?' asked Dantar.

'By the look of his epitaph, he was a swindler.'

The panel was held in place by a simple latch, and Marko quickly had it open. Dantar helped him lift out the coffin. Removing the lid, they saw that Feldinius Aclar had been dead a very long time.

'No purse,' said Marko, rummaging amid the bones and crumbling cloth. 'Still, someone like him would definitely try to take his money with him . . . Ah! I knew it. See here!'

Just below the ribs were several small gold coins.

'He must have swallowed them on his deathbed,' said Dantar. 'Clever. That way the relatives, undertakers and deathwalkers missed out on the last of his loot.'

'Three, four, five coins. Small, but real gold. Savarian moonlets.'

'What is this place?' asked Dantar.

'These are the crypts,' said Merikus. 'The bodies are carried down here in coffins by the priests and relatives. After fifty years the bones are tossed, the coffins are re-used, and the cover is painted over for the next body.'

He waved a little paw at a stack of coffins. Dantar and Marko put Feldinius back in his crypt and secured the latch.

'Well, time we were —' began Marko, before a flicker of green light behind them cut him short.

'Hiding,' said Dantar. 'That must be Avantar, though I thought he drowned.'

'Not human,' said Marko, as he lifted the lid of a coffin. 'Hurry, choose one and get in.'

'I'll just be a rat and lurk about,' said Merikus.

Dantar waited in darkness. The smell was not at all bad compared to the reek of the sewers, just a vaguely unpleasant mustiness. Presently he heard footsteps padding along the crypt chamber, before they receded into the distance. Suddenly there were cries of alarm, and green light glowed through the cracks in the wood of the ancient coffin. Dantar lay still for a time, then raised the lid a little. All was silent, but there was the glow of a fire in the distance. He tapped at Marko's coffin.

'Safe to go,' he said.

'Pity, I was enjoying the rest,' said Marko.

Merikus came scampering from the direction of the fire.

'That twin of yours, he just flamed a dozen deathwalkers in their tearoom!' squeaked the rat. 'You should see it, charred bodies and burning furniture all over the place.'

'They must have tried to stop him,' said Marko. 'The Deathwalkers' Guild doesn't allow visitors down here. I was going to use those gold coins to pay the fine that they would have charged.'

'Well, he's left now,' said Merikus. 'Time we were leaving too.'

They passed a stone chamber where the remains of tables, chairs and wooden chests were still smouldering. Burnt bodies lay everywhere.

'The deathwalkers won't like that,' said Merikus. 'They take badly to having their own folk killed.'

'Well then, why not give the survivors a clue?' said Dantar, and taking the charred leg of a chair, he wrote AVANTAR on the wall in charcoal.

They followed Avantar's trail, made up of the burning ruins of doors and the occasional deathwalker's body. At last they found themselves in a temple, and saw that the sky outside was dark. Thinking that the air smelled sweeter than the perfume of the great courtly ladies, Dantar stood there breathing deeply for some moments.

'Come along, plenty of time for breathing later,' said Marko, then he dropped to one knee before Merikus. 'Prince Merikus, thank you for your service. You have been a rat of your word.'

'My thanks, too,' said Dantar grudgingly, although he did not kneel. 'Farewell, now.'

'Wait! Wait!' squeaked Merikus. 'I want to go with you.'

'Told you!' exclaimed Marko, turning to

Dantar. 'He's that shapeshifter dragon that's been protecting you.'

'Yeah! Yeah! I'm your dragon!' squeaked Merikus. 'Take me with you.'

'You're a rat and you're lying,' said Dantar.

'How can you tell?' asked Marko.

'He's a *rat*,' Dantar said.

'Please, please, I don't want to spend the rest of my life down there,' pleaded Merikus. 'All I ever get to eat is rotten garbage and there's always poo on it. The conversation's not much either, like there's only rats down there. All I've got is a pipe to sleep in.'

'I want a bath,' said Marko. 'We have to visit a bathhouse, but first we need a night market where I can change one of these little gold coins into silver and buy us clean clothes and food. We can't afford to draw attention to ourselves by walking about in rags and smelling like sewage.'

'So can I come with you?' asked Merikus.

'Only if you have a bath too,' said Dantar.

The youths attracted a lot of stares at the night market, but they had no trouble changing a gold coin into twelve silver nobles. They then bought new clothes and found a bathhouse. The rags that they had been wearing went straight into a garbage basket, and soon they were clean, and relaxing in a pair of stone baths.

'Never used soap before, only ate it,' said Merikus as he sat on the edge of Dantar's bath, rubbing soap into his fur.

'I'll buy a phial of asperbalm oil once we're dry and dressed,' said Marko. 'The cuts and scratches we got in the sewers might get inflamed and cause us to have fevers otherwise.'

'Could that thing have really been my brother?' Dantar wondered aloud.

'Didn't seem human to me,' said Merikus. 'Did you notice how his awkward speech improved while he talked to you?'

The rat jumped into Dantar's bathwater and paddled about. Dantar lay back and folded his arms.

'If he *was* my brother, he's worse than my sister,' he decided.

'He's not your brother, Dantar,' said Marko.

'He's probably a shapecasting.'

'But he would have to be a shapecasting of earth, fire, water and air. That's forbidden magic.'

'Just because something's forbidden, doesn't mean people will not try to do it. Calbaras must have made him. Few warlocks today have that kind of power. Of course, he'd have needed something from you. Did you give him something? Blood, a bit of fingernail —'

'My hair!' exclaimed Dantar, as a tiny detail from the meeting with his father fell into place. 'He plucked one of my hairs!'

'Blood is better, but anything will do. He could use that to control you, too.'

'He tried.'

Marko frowned. 'He did? What happened?'

'I don't know. I was able to throw his casting off somehow.'

Marko's frown deepened. 'That's unusual.'

'You seem to know a lot about magic for a common sailor. Are you sure it was all from reading stolen books?'

'I know enough of shapecasting theory to keep alive. Some of what I know tells me that *you* are very special,' Marko said.

'*Him, special?*' muttered Merikus, climbing up onto Dantar's knee. 'If you ask me –'

'I'd rather not,' said Dantar, who then submerged his knees, forcing Merikus to swim away.

'You're the son of a warlock, but with no magic at all. Suddenly your twin appears, a shapecasting with all four magics. I wish I could work it out, but it's very advanced magic. Something strange is going on – and while we're on the subject, you're special too, Merikus.'

'Me? Why?'

'You are a shapeshifted something.'

'I am not!'

'Yes you are. Rats are too small to support a human spirit. Dragons . . . nobody knows what dragons can do if they really try. Do you have any memories of a mother about the size of a ship?'

'Absolutely not! I was always like this.'

'How long is always?'

'A year or two, I suppose. I sort of lost track of time, after I escaped into the sewers.'

'Escaped?'

'I was kept in a cage with some other rats, and

a human did things to us. We lived in a room full of bottles, books, glass tubes and other things that I didn't understand. Every so often a human with a beard, long robes and a pointy hat would take one of us out and do things to us. Some of us died, but some of us learned to understand human speech. I was special, I learned to talk, too.'

'Sounds like a warlock,' said Dantar. 'Why did he use rats for his tests?'

'I once heard him talking to a visitor, and he said he could test forbidden magic on rats because they are too small for dragons to detect. He made me say "good evening, Lord Calbaras" to the visitor.'

Dantar and Marko glanced at each other.

'Are you sure it was Calbaras?' asked Marko.

'As sure as a rat can be. Lord Calbaras called him Torvoran.'

'Torvoran is not a Savarian name. He may be some foreign wizard or warlock, who is doing secret work in Teliz, where he is not known.'

'And he and my father are comparing results by the sound of it,' said Dantar.

'How did you escape?' Marko asked Merikus.

'One day the warlock cast a spell on my friend Scattle and me together, so we would understand Dravinian as well. It worked, but he was so exhausted that he fell asleep in a chair. He had us in a tall glass jar. It was too tall for a rat to climb out of, but I climbed on Scattle's shoulders and reached the lip of the jar. I then pushed the jar off the table so Scattle could escape. The warlock woke up and chased us when the jar smashed, but we escaped down the privy.'

'So, Calbaras is not working on the forbidden magics alone,' said Marko.

'You know Calbaras?' asked Merikus suspiciously.

'He's no friend,' said Dantar.

For a while they said nothing. Dantar tried to recall his own early childhood. There were birthday parties, lessons from tutors, and occasional beatings for doing things like putting a frog in his sister's bed, but there were a lot of gaps as well. Too many gaps to be put down to just poor memory. *Might I too have been used for tests, just like Merikus and Scattle?* he wondered. *No, can't have been. I'm bigger than a rat, so the dragons would sense me.*

'So what now?' he asked, noticing that the bath water was getting cold.

'We dry ourselves, dress in our new clothes and return to the night market,' said Marko. 'Now that we're clean, nobody will recognise us. We can eat, buy packs and supplies, then . . . weapons! We can buy weapons and pass ourselves off as mercenaries, then tell the guards at the city gates that we're going home because the war is over.'

'Is it?'

'Who knows? Trust me, Dantar, guards on gates are far more anxious to keep armed foreigners out of a city than to bother stopping them leaving. Actually, we should buy a horse, too.'

'A horse? That will cost another gold moonlet. Why do we need a horse?'

'We're going to Port Regent, and it's a hundred miles up the coast.'

DRAGONS

'*The chick has reappeared, and I sense great contentment*,' said Videnveld as she glided above the centre of Teliz with Grimvaud.

'*He must have been underground*,' replied Grimvaud. '*Too much earth, it smothers what it is that makes us dragons.*'

'*We should rescue him.*'

'*No! If he is contented, he is not in danger. Remember what we agreed? The chick must be studied. This is no ordinary spawn of dragons. We must learn where it came from, and the path of its bloodline.*'

'*Then a council must be called. Adulteration of bloodlines cannot be tolerated.*'

'*I shall go and begin the calling,*' said Grimvaud. '*Stay with the dragonling, but do not descend unless it is in the most dire of perils.*'

Grimvaud banked steeply, and with great,

ponderous beats of his wings, flew out over the dark ocean. On the following morning the people of the city looked up to see that there were no dragons circling high over the city. Bells were rung, gongs boomed, and people flocked into temples to give thanks that the danger looming over them had vanished.

Crowds gathered before the palace spontaneously to cheer the king, for now the last two dragons were gone. While King Lavarran did not take credit for saving the city, he had the good sense not to deny it, either. Appearing on a palace balcony in gold-plated armour, and with his crown-helmet under one arm, he smiled, waved, and acknowledged the cheers.

VELZA

Castles are built for strength. They are meant to keep armies out, even if those armies have battering rams and catapults. Palaces are built to be impressive and comfortable, and are generally inside cities. That means the city walls keep the invading armies out. Unfortunately that also means that an angry mob of citizens from inside the city can attack a palace with a fairly good chance of gaining access, but that gives the ruling monarch some incentive to rule wisely, not tax too heavily, and make sure that the garbage is collected and the streets are swept.

Palaces do have a lot of guards, however. On any one day there are always dozens of angry, revolutionary, or just plain crazy people who would like nothing better than to kill the king. Of course this means that the parts of the palace where the king lives and works are more heavily guarded than the royal stables or coach house. The dungeons are another matter yet again, because they are meant to keep people in, rather than out.

The forecourt of the royal palace of Teliz was a wide area paved with cobblestones, where coaches would draw up and visiting dignitaries step out. There was a grand balcony above the main doors, so that the king could look down on visitors as they arrived and force them to look up at him, but on this day the forecourt was being used for a farewell.

Two bodies of hounds lay on top of a pile of firewood soaked in lamp oil. One of them was a troll hound that Stormvaud had found in the prison castle, but the other was one of Lavarran's over-fed pets. The other troll hound from the prison castle was nearby, securely locked away.

The pyre was surrounded by guards. King Lavarran and two mercenaries looked down from the balcony and checked that all was in order, then the monarch raised a hand and gestured in the direction of the dead hounds. A guard walked forward with a burning torch, applied it to the base of the pyre, then retreated quickly as the flames flared up and took hold.

'There should be quite a show when the magic is released from the troll hound's body,' said Latsar. 'Usually it just ebbs away slowly as the body rots and becomes one with the earth.'

'So the other troll hound is in my prison tower?' asked the king.

'Yes, in a vat of vinegar. Can't have it rotting.'

'And are you sure that Calbaras will mistake it for Dantar and try to break in?'

'I am not sure of anything, your Majesty,' said Velza, 'but Calbaras does seem to value Dantar for some reason.'

'Very opportune that someone managed to poison one of my hounds just when we needed a second dead dog, don't you think so, Latsar?'

'Lady Fortune does appear to have smiled upon us, brother. What with all that fat, it should burn very nicely.'

'Would you happen to know anything about it, brother?'

'Not unless my name is Lady Fortune.'

'You are always talking about making your own luck, so perhaps the name is not such a bad fit —'

He was cut short by a flash of blue fire that blazed out from the funeral pyre, then became a great blue cloud that rose into the air and drifted away in the direction of the sea.

'Water,' said Velza. 'I've read about this but never seen it happen. When dragons die, you can see the colours of the four magics liberated.'

'When that dragon hit the mountain it only flashed white,' said Lavarran.

'White light is made of all colours, your Majesty. You see that in rainbows, when sunlight is split up by raindrops.'

Now the pyre was wreathed in a shimmer of gold. Slowly the wavering air became a column over the blaze, and this suddenly shot up into the sky like the bolt from a giant crossbow.

'Air's power has been released,' said Velza.

Green light now radiated from the blaze, then there was a loud whoosh and a torus of brownish red expanded away from the flames and was absorbed by the walls and buildings.

'The power of earth, returning to earth,' explained Velza.

'So fire will be just fire?' asked the king.

'I expect so, your Majesty, but —'

The pyre suddenly became smothered in what seemed like a writhing ball of green ropes, and as they watched, the ropes seemed to tie themselves tighter and tighter. They contracted down to a tiny green point of light that blazed as brilliantly as the sun, then it exploded like a thunderclap, shattering every window that faced the forecourt and knocking most of the guards off their feet.

'– but you never can tell with dragon magic,' Velza concluded.

Down in the forecourt there were only some scorches on the cobblestones to show where the fire had been. Not even ash remained.

'What next?' asked Latsar as he got to his feet.

'Now Calbaras will think that the only creature in the city that is tainted by dragon magic is Dantar. He must be able to sense dragon magic, so he will think that Dantar is locked away in your dungeon tower.'

'So your brother really is magical?' asked the king.

'No, but my brother seems to be protected by a very powerful spell, the same type that shapeshifted the two hounds. Calbaras will not know it is a hound pickled in vinegar that we have locked in that tower –'

There was a distant scream of rage, then green flames blasted out of one of the upper windows of the tower, melting the bars. These were followed by a laundry vat and a body.

'Until he breaks in!' exclaimed Latsar. 'Hurry.'

Leaving the king on the balcony, Velza and Latsar ran down the stairs and sprinted across the forecourt and past the stables to the base of the tower. Several bodies of guards lay scattered in front of the door, which had literally been burned open. Nearby lay a smashed wooden vat, the body of a hound, and a great deal of spilled vinegar. Someone had been very angry about being tricked.

'How did he get past the main gate?' asked Velza as they stopped before the door.

'I'd say he used a delivery gate, which is probably now a smoking hole in the wall, surrounded by dead guards,' said Latsar. 'How did he get so far without being noticed?'

'He saw our preparations to burn the hounds through the bars of the main gate, along with every citizen of Teliz that walked past. He knew how dramatic the cremation would be, so he attacked while we were all distracted.'

At that moment a figure appeared in the doorway.

'Dantar!' exclaimed Velza and Latsar together.

The figure turned to them, his eyes blazing with anger and hate. As he opened his mouth, they saw a green glow blazing within his throat.

Because she was a fire shapecaster, Velza was able to cast a fire shield in time to make the flames splash sideways and away from her and Latsar. The fury of the flames sent her staggering back, and she had a fleeting glimpse of a small youth dashing away before she collapsed from the strain of holding the casting together.

She shook her head as Latsar helped her up.

'What is this?' he asked. 'Did Calbaras send Dantar to abduct Dantar?'

'That thing was not my little brother, Latsar. Calbaras appears to have mastered the four magics so well that he has created a thing with a dragon's powers in a human body.'

'Imagine what an army of those creatures could do.'

'I know. They would have dragon powers without dragon wisdom, and we would have to fight the war of the Dark Hands all over again.'

Just then a squad of guardsmen appeared in the distance. Latsar waved a coded signal at them, and they approached warily.

'Lavarran will be somewhere behind all those guards,' said Latsar. 'What do we tell him?'

'Your brother must warn the other kingdoms, and the dragons. Everyone must go after Calbaras and not start fighting among themselves.'

'Did you notice that the dragons have flown away?'

'Yes, but at least we know that Calbaras does not have Dantar. Dantar is the key to everything, but we have no idea what he opens. Perhaps he is a living book of forbidden knowledge. He could be the spark that ignites the worst war this world has seen for a thousand years.'

DANTAR

Dantar and Marko left through the northwest gate of Teliz, and set out along the coast road. When asked why they were leaving so late at night, Marko explained that they had been ordered to set up a checkpoint a mile down the road. The guards were skeptical, but a lot of disruption had been caused by the recent fighting, so they were waved through.

Now they set about putting as much distance as they could between themselves and Teliz. The youths saw no sign of pursuit, but Dantar had a nagging feeling that his dark twin would soon be following them. They took turns sleeping as the horse plodded along steadily through the starlit darkness. By dawn they were approaching a coastal hamlet.

'The horse will need to get some sleep,' said

Dantar after shaking Marko awake.

Marko yawned. 'It will get all the sleep it wants in this hamlet. Meantime we shall be on a fresh horse, travelling on. The city's only about twenty miles behind us.'

They were approaching their third village, a little fishing port, when the weather changed. Although it was high summer, a storm front was approaching. The birds and rabbits had already taken shelter, and jagged lightning lashed across the sky, out over the sea.

'A cold front,' said Dantar, pointing to the west where the setting sun was obscured by clouds.

'We're nearly in the tropics,' said Marko. 'You don't get cold fronts here.'

'Then what?'

'We're travelling by day and night, and are over halfway to Port Regent. That's good progress.'

'And I'm sick of sleeping on horseback.'

'But your evil twin, Avantar, is probably having trouble keeping up. I think he's raised a tropical storm to force us off the road to find shelter.'

'It never rains in the sewers,' said Merikus from Marko's pocket.

'If you want to go back to them you can get off

and walk back to Teliz,' said Dantar.

'Actually, we're going to get off and walk now,' said Marko.

'What? Back to Teliz?'

'No, to that little fishing village up ahead, but first we'll turn the horse loose in the woodlands off to the right.'

'You're planning something.'

'If I'm not planning something, I'm asleep,' Marko said. 'It costs way less to take salted fish to market by sea, and I can see the masts of a coastal trader up ahead, at the village.'

'From this distance?'

'Yes!' Marko threw up his hands in exasperation. 'It's just too big to be a fishing boat. It will be going to Port Regent and it will sail in about an hour – Stop! Don't ask me how I know, think it through for yourself.'

They dismounted, led the horse into the woodlands and set it free to graze, out of sight from the road. Marko also had them hide the swords and helmets they had bought in Teliz, and cut quarterstaffs from saplings. As they walked on to the fishing village, Dantar pretended that he was alone, and that his survival depended on thinking through everything for himself.

'The ship sails in an hour because the villagers would load it during daylight, and it can travel to the next fishing port by night,' he said.

'Very good,' said Marko.

'And the sun is setting, and Moon is near the sun, so there will be a tide change to take it out to sea.'

'Close enough.'

'When Avantar reaches this place he will ask if two mercenaries on one horse have passed this way. The villagers will say no, because we *walked* in, and we carry no weapons or armour. He will think we saw the storm coming and left the road to find shelter before reaching the village. He will then do a shapecasting to call off the storm and wait at the village.'

'Well done. Now how do I know that the ship up ahead is not going to Teliz?'

'Er, there's a war going on?'

'Close.'

'All the ships in Teliz harbour have been burned or stolen . . . but that means ships will be in demand, lots of cargo to be carried. Wait a moment, that's a good reason to go there.'

'Well thought, but think some more.'

'No ships in Teliz . . . Oh, I see. The king will be seizing everything that floats and putting marines aboard in case we Dravinians come back for another attack. The fighting was about five days ago, and that's enough time for word to spread this far along the coast.'

'So there you have it! Nothing magical about my decisions, and no guesswork involved.'

'But lots of savvy thinking. You're a lot more than a sailor, aren't you?'

'So? You're a lot more than a cabin boy turned junior officer. You're the son of a powerful warlock, and have even been a pageboy in the Dravinian royal court. Who would guess it?'

'And what are you?'

'War is bad for trade, because those who have lost have had all their goods looted, and those who have won have all the loot. That means nobody buying or selling. People like me are employed by merchants to keep an eye on who is fighting who, and where. That way people who own ships can send them somewhere else.'

That made some sense to Dantar. It explained how Marko knew where the coastal trader was liable to be sailing, yet Dantar still had the feeling that his friend was not telling the whole truth.

'You could find all that out by asking any ship's rat,' squeaked Merikus.

'Except that I don't speak rat,' said Marko.

Rain had begun to fall by the time they reached the village, so nobody was out or about as they made their way to the single pier where the coastal trader was tied up. When they reached the ship, however, the captain of the two-master told them he was taking no passengers.

'The king's press gangs have taken three sailors out of every four for his bleeding war,' he said accusingly, as if Dantar or Marko were the king. 'There's only me and four old sailors to sail this thing, so a pair of young louts like you two could take us over once we're at sea.'

'But we're not armed, and your ship is only carrying salt fish,' said Marko.

'The answer's no. Anyway, we're not sailing tonight. Not enough men to sail this thing through that approaching rainstorm.'

'We're sailors, and we're young and strong,' said Dantar. 'If you let us work our passage you can sail right away.'

'You're sailors? Yet you walked here?'

'All the ships in Teliz harbour were burned or stolen by the Dravinians, so we're out of work. We were walking to Port Regent to look for employment, but when we saw your ship we thought you might need hands.'

'Tie me a reef knot,' said the captain, holding out a length of rope.

Marko took the rope and tied the knot. Several knots and questions later, the ship cast off with two extra sailors aboard. Although they were in the rainstorm for the first few hours, by midnight they had sailed clear of it and the following morning saw the ship tied up and loading yet more fish at the next port. Marko and Dantar joined in with the villagers who were loading the ship, so that by noon they were at sea again, and the next stop was Port Regent.

VELZA

There were higher priorities for the city authorities in Teliz than rebuilding the prison castle at the edge of the city, so very little had been done there since the dragon Stormvaud had ripped the top of the building apart. The dead who could be reached without too much effort had been carted away and buried, the stone blocks that were in the way had been dragged aside, and the surviving guards went on guarding the surviving prisoners.

Velza had a royal pass to go wherever she wished, as long as she was under escort by Latsar, and the guards looked on with curiosity as they climbed over the piles of rubble and stone blocks.

'Tell me again why we are here,' said Latsar as Velza inspected a stone block that had a groove scratched in it by a giant talon.

'I'm searching for these,' she replied, peering closely at the groove. 'I need traces of dragon.'

'Well, that groove in the stone is a pretty strong trace.'

'The groove is what he did. I want to find bits of him. Dragons are real things bound together by magical energies. Even though they are very tough, tiny bits do break off sometimes, and those bits have the magic of all four elements. Father used to have a little jar of chips from a dragon's claw, and he said the fragments were worth their weight in diamonds.'

'Okay, where are the chips?'

'That's what I want to know. These grooves are so clean you would think they had been scrubbed.'

Latsar beckoned to a nearby guard.

'These stone blocks, the ones that the dragon clawed,' he said. 'Has anyone been near them since the dragon flew off?'

'Have they what, m'lord!' replied the guard. 'The place was swarming with wizards and their apprentices almost as soon as the rubble stopped falling.'

'I see. Could you identify any of them?'

By noon a dozen wizards had been strung up by their thumbs in the palace forecourt, with their feet resting on piles of brushwood stakes. Their apprentices stood watching, each chained to a guard. King Lavarran paced before them, his hands clasped behind his back.

'So far I have been reasonable,' he declared. 'You have all been identified as having removed material from royal property, that is, the stones of the prison castle. By law, anything adhering to those stones, be it bird droppings or diamonds, is my property, just as surely as the deer in the royal forest are my property. The penalty for poaching deer is death, but as this is the first case of dragon claw chips being stolen, I am willing to grant a royal pardon to all those who hand over what was stolen. Who wishes to tell my guards where they have hidden the chips they stole?'

All twelve wizards did a good job of looking terrified, and several swore that they had never been near the prison castle. None confessed to the theft.

'Very well, burn that one with the broad chest,

he looks as if he can scream the loudest.'

A guard with a burning torch touched the flame to the pile of brushwood at the wizard's feet. At first he seemed to be trying to dance a jig in the flames, and the lower part of his robe was on fire before he screamed the location of the contraband dragon claw chips. Several guards who had been standing ready with pails of water doused the flames.

'Next!' said the king, pointing to another wizard.

This man immediately confessed the location of his jar of chips, and only two more of the remaining wizards had to be set on fire to make them give up their windfall treasures. Even so, the combined weight of the claw chips was about that of perhaps three or four grains of sand.

Velza needed the highest tower in the palace for her shapecasting. King Lavarran allowed only Latsar and himself to be present.

'I am not sure that I approve of how these were collected,' said Velza as she gently placed the chips on a tray of gold leaf the size of a fingernail.

'By law the wizards should have been executed,' said Lavarran. 'I let them off very lightly.'

'Three of them will not be walking anywhere for a month or so.'

'Then their apprentices can do the walking. What are you doing?'

'Dragon magic seeks out dragon magic. Calbaras has mastered some elements of dragon magic, so he resembles a dragon in the same way that a painting of me resembles me. That means the tray of fragments will be able to see Calbaras if I perform a casting upon them.'

Velza began to chant, but it was a very advanced casting and it collapsed several times before the pile of fragments shapeshifted into the image of a tiny dragon. Looking down at it through a glass magnifier, she spoke her question.

'Is any creature of earth, air, fire and water within the city?'

The tiny image raised a winged arm and pointed. Velza noted the direction.

'May I see?' asked Lavarran.

Velza handed him the magnifier, then looked out across the city. The dragon had pointed in the general direction of the docks, but directly between the palace and the docks was a Deathlight tower.

'How long will this creature live?' asked Lavarran as he gazed down at the perfectly formed little dragon through the magnifier.

'An hour's half, your Majesty, when the claw fragments will become dust. Please, we need to go in search of Calbaras.'

'Take Latsar and a dozen guards,' said the king, without looking up. 'This little dragon is wonderful! How can I make him do tricks, like breathe fire?'

'I shall write out some simple commands, before I go,' said Velza.

Velza and Latsar began the long descent of the tower.

'Calbaras is in one of the Deathlight towers,' said Velza.

'That will cause problems. The secrets of

Deathlight are guarded more closely than the king's meals.'

'That has to be why Calbaras is hiding there!' Velza exclaimed. 'We must have a search made.'

'That will be difficult to arrange,' said Latsar. 'Those doing the searching will have to be operators who understand the Deathlight mechanism. They will have to be recruited from other towers, and palace guards will have to surround the base of the tower to stop anyone escaping.'

'How long will that take?'

'Days, most likely.'

'What? Calbaras could just walk out and be anywhere by then. Can the king get it done any faster?'

'Yes, he's King, after all,' said Latsar as they reached the bottom of the stairway.

'Then get me a squad of guards to surround the tower, then go back up to Lavarran and get his permission to get the operators from the other towers.'

'What? All that way? You could have told me before we started down.'

Velza marched from the palace at the head of two dozen guards, carrying a scroll with the royal seal. The tower was surrounded with no warning at all, and the duty captain was presented with a scroll granting admission to Velza, and commanding the duty captain to give her total cooperation while she searched the tower.

An hour later Velza was back in the palace, locked in a cell in Miscreant Tower.

King Lavarran put his hand between the bars of Velza's cell. Slowly, reluctantly, Velza took the copy of the royal seal ring from her purse and placed it on his palm. Lavarran now turned to Latsar and held out his hand again.

'She borrowed my only copy,' said Latsar.

The king snapped his fingers and pointed to Latsar. Two guards advanced and seized the prince.

'Strip him naked, here and now,' said Lavarran, 'then search his clothing until you find his other copy.'

'Can I watch?' asked Velza.

'Nothing much to see,' said Lavarran.

'Now just a moment –' began Latsar.

'The ring, brother of mine, give it here!' demanded Lavarran. 'Your copy of my ring.'

Latsar reached into his robes, then tossed the ring to Lavarran.

'Now then, Lady Velza, also known as the Iron Claw,' Lavarran continued, 'you are currently the only Dravinian who has seen the secrets of a Deathlight mechanism. What am I to do with you?'

'I was only searching for my father. If he had been in the tower he might have escaped if we had followed official procedures.'

'If. But he was not in the tower, was he?'

'Er, no. Your Majesty.'

'And your trick with the teeny dragon might have been part of a scheme to gain access to the tower to learn Deathlight's secrets for the Dravinian emperor.'

'It does indeed look that way,' Velza admitted.

'Well then, I shall have to keep you here for quite some time, I'm afraid. The cell is designed to hold fire shapecasters, so don't bother trying to flame your way out. I do quite like you, so consider yourself my guest. You may have anything you wish: books, clothes, the food of your choice, and so on. Just don't ask for the key.'

DANTAR

Dantar had been feeling unhappy because everything was going really well. He was not a very optimistic sort of person, and believed that any run of stunningly good luck would soon be balanced by a run of luck that was catastrophically bad. Once they were at sea again, he was almost relieved when the bad luck started to balance things back in its direction.

'I've been talking to the ship's rats,' Merikus reported as the two youths ate their lunch. 'They said that there are press gangs in Port Regent who have seized all the Savarian ships bigger than this thing. Anyone looking like a sailor is being caught, put aboard a confiscated ship and sworn into the king's navy.'

'That's the first constructive thing you've said in days,' said Dantar.

'There's more. Didn't you think the captain changed his tune a bit too quickly when you said you were sailors?'

'Well yes, but the ship is badly undermanned,' said Marko. 'Anyone who knows the difference between a mast and a rudder can see that.'

'And there's a bounty for anyone turning in a sailor to the press gangs. You two will give the captain a nice little bonus for this voyage.'

Marko thought about this while he finished his lunch.

'The sailors are all pretty old,' said Dantar. 'We could fight our way off.'

'And the press gangs would be waiting for you as you fight your way down the gangplank,' said Merikus.

'Dantar, you really need to learn how to swim,' said Marko, 'but for now these will have to do.'

He handed Dantar what seemed like two very light wooden boards. 'I put these aside especially for you.'

'What have they to do with swimming?' Dantar asked.

'They are the bark of the cork tree, they float even better than wood. Tie these to your chest and back under your tunic, and you will be able to swim as well as me. At Port Regent we will slip over the side and swim for any ship that's not flying a Savarian pennant.'

When they reached Port Regent the captain told them to stay aboard while he sold his cargo and collected the money for their wages. As soon as he was off the ship, Dantar and Marko climbed over the seaward side and swam under the pier until they reached a ship flying the pennant of the Secaster Archipelago. Here they climbed up onto the pier, then hid behind crates and sacks until they saw the captain of the coastal trader march past at the head of a press gang. Only now did they hurry aboard the Secasteran vessel.

'Well done,' said the captain in Savarian. 'I saw you two swimming along under the pier.'

'Need a couple of sailors?' asked Marko.

'Everyone needs sailors, what with the press gangs catching everyone under sixty who can haul on a rope or tie a knot. We're sailing for the Dravinian colony of Merk, on Crondar. I think you will want to go there.'

'Ah, why is that?' asked Marko.

'Because you speak Savarian with a Dravinian

accent, meaning that you're probably Dravinian sailors who had the ship sunk from under you at the Battle of Teliz. My terms are meals with no wages in return for working the ten days it will take to reach Merk. This will make me a little more money than selling you to the press gangs.'

'How do you know all this about us?' asked Dantar.

'Because another nine Dravinian sailors are hiding below. If you two join them I'll have enough crewmen to put to sea. Do we have an agreement?'

'If it's good enough for the other nine, it's good enough for us,' said Marko. 'When do you sail?'

'As soon as I can get everyone on deck and cast off! When that press gang finishes searching the coastal trader and finds that you're not there, they're going to search all nearby ships.'

The Secasteran ship turned out to be a poor choice — if they had had a choice. The ten-day voyage lasted four weeks, because the winds died away on the Tropic of Solstice. Food had to be rationed, small wriggling things were living in the water, and the tropical sun baked the ship like a loaf of bread in an oven. Worse, the ship only had enough provisions for a ten-day crossing.

Merikus recruited some of the ship's rats to steal food for them from the kitchen stores, but there was not much of it, and the quality was poor.

'I'm not happy about eating ship's biscuit that's been carried in a rat's mouth,' said Dantar. 'Besides, it's as hard as stone.'

'Break it up with the handle of your knife,' said Marko.

Dantar got to work, but stopped after a few moments.

'Oi, there's maggots in this biscuit!' he exclaimed.

'Well, you wouldn't want to eat something that the maggots would not touch. Give them here.'

Marko picked out the maggots from the crumbs of ship's biscuit and popped them into his mouth.

'I don't believe my eyes, you're eating maggots!' exclaimed Dantar.

'They're delicious.'

'They're revolting.'

'Do you like honey?'

'Yes.'

'It's bees' vomit.'

'What? You're making that up.'

'No I'm not. Now eat your crumbs, and if you find any more maggots, hand them over.'

At last the lookout shouted that the Crondarian coast was in sight. The captain ordered a dozen of the crew into a gigboat, and they slowly towed the ship to catch a coastal current that the navigator knew about. Two days later they were finally tied up in Merk, and the Dravinian sailors could not leave fast enough. Dantar and Marko made straight for the nearest tavern and spent two silver Savarian nobles on pies and ale.

They said little as they ate, but before long the Secasteran captain came in and announced that he was recruiting Savarian sailors at double pay for a voyage to Port Regent.

'A good scheme,' said Dantar through a mouthful of pie. 'He recruits Dravinian sailors in Port Regent, doesn't pay them, feeds them garbage, then replaces them with Savarian sailors here in Merk and sells them to the press gangs in Port Regent before he pays their wages.'

'Welcome to life at sea,' replied Marko.

'Yo ho ho,' muttered Dantar.

'Any pie crusts going to waste?' called Merikus from Marko's pocket.

VELZA

If you are going to be locked up, the Savarian royal palace was a good place to be. Velza's cell was in Miscreant Tower, the penal tower of the palace. It was comfortably furnished, the meals were good, and there was a window with an excellent view of the harbour and the Deathlight tower that she had so rashly searched. As the weeks passed Velza saw the galley fleet return, and the gradual buildup of merchant ships that had been seized for the Savarian navy. Although the docks had been damaged by both the dragon and Captain Parvian's raid, all the repair work was being put into the ships.

This made sense. The Dravinian fleet had been badly mauled in the Battle of Teliz, and would have sailed to the island of Morticas for repairs. Certainly the ships that Parvian had stolen from Teliz were headed there. They would not be expecting to be chased, so the Savarians could wipe out the Dravinian navy in a second battle.

As comfortable as Velza's cell was, there was no opportunity for breaking out. The walls were stone, the roof was arched with bricks, the door was solid iron and the windows had iron bars. Even the floor was made from marble flagstones. Every day she searched the cell for some vulnerability, and twenty-seven times she found none.

'Definitely designed to hold a fire shapecaster,' she muttered as she checked the cell for some possible means of escape for the twenty-eighth time.

As usual, the key to the door remained the only way out, and that key was now kept by the king. Velza browsed a new book that had been sent from the king's library. After a few pages she realised that it was about a princess locked in a tower. She turned to the last page.

'Sure enough, rescued by a knight on a magical flying horse,' she said, then pushed the book between the bars of the window. After some moments a thud echoed up from the pathway below.

She thought through what had gone wrong with her shapecasting to find Calbaras four weeks earlier. The tiny dragon she had conjured had pointed at the Deathlight tower, yet the warlock had not been there. She looked at the tower through the bars of the window . . . and beyond that the docks. Suddenly she had it. Calbaras might have been hiding somewhere in the docks. There were no fragments of dragon claw left, yet there was another way to locate the warlock: she was of the same blood as him.

She snapped her fingers above a candle, and a yellow flame popped into life on the wick. Plucking a hair, she dropped it into the flame and chanted a spell of affinity as it sizzled and smoked. She twirled her finger around the flame, and it now bent in her direction. That was good, it had been charged to seek her out. She passed her finger through the flame, cancelling the link to herself.

Now the flame stood straight up again . . . but not quite. There was a slight angle in the enchanted flame as it sought out Velza's bloodline. It was inclining in the direction of the window. She looked through the window. The flame was pointing to the docks, just as the shapecast dragon had. Someone of her bloodline was there. Dantar? Her dragon image would not have seen Dantar, because he had no magic at all. The copy of Dantar? It had no real blood. It had to be Calbaras who was attracting the flame.

Velza called for the guard and asked to see Latsar. She waited the entire day, and the sun had long set before Latsar arrived.

'Calbaras is at the docks,' Velza said as soon as he arrived. 'I performed the bloodline flame spell this morning. It pointed to him, just as the dragon did.'

'You said he was in that Deathlight tower,' said Latsar.

'I was wrong! The docks are behind that tower.'

'Fine try, Velza, but you stay behind bars. You now know so much about the Deathlight machines that we can't let you go.'

'Even to save your warlocks, wizards and shapecasters?'

'What do you mean?'

'Your fleet is being readied to chase the Dravinian fleet. There will be another battle. This time the fleets will annihilate each other, and the cream of the Savarian and Dravinian shapecasters will die. Calbaras will make sure of that. Our friend Pandas is on the Dravinian fleet, have you forgotten him? He will die too.'

'How do you know Calbaras's plans?'

'I don't, but if Calbaras is with the Savarian fleet he is sure to have a plan.'

Latsar thought about this for a moment. Finally he shrugged and spread his arms wide.

'Very well, can you show me your bloodline casting?'

'Bloodline flame spell. Just a moment.'

Latsar watched through the bars as Velza lit the candle again, spoke the spell words and burned a hair in the flame. This time the flame stood straight up after she passed her finger through it.

'Am I missing something?' asked Latsar.

'If Calbaras were deep under the city, earth would smother his fire bloodline,' said Velza. 'If he ventures more than a day's journey away my flame could not find him either. How could he be underground yet at the docks?'

'He might have sailed with the fleet,' Latsar suggested.

'Sailed?' said Velza. 'Did you just say *sailed*?'

'That I did. The fleet sailed tonight, just after dark, for secrecy. Can't be too careful with spies like you about.'

'No! Calbaras has some plan to wipe out every magical warrior except himself. The fleet must be called back.'

'That can't be done. The king sent it out on an invariant order. That means his fleet can't get new orders unless it destroys the Dravinian fleet or captures the Dravinian island of Morticas. Patrol hawks will kill any messenger bird sent after it, even from the king's own coop.'

Velza slumped back in her cell's chair.

'Then it's too late,' said Velza. 'My father will finish the slaughter he started at the Battle of Teliz.'

DANTAR

Dantar and Marko had been noticed as they left the ship in Merk. The interest in them continued as they spent Savarian silver in the tavern, and it absolutely blossomed as they returned to the docks and asked whether two Savarian gold moonlets would buy them passage home to Haldan, in Dravinia.

They were young sailors, just off a ship. That meant they had probably been paid. They spent Savarian money, implying that they did not know the port of Merk very well. When they offered gold to travel to Dravinia, they were summarised as foolish young foreigners who carried bags of gold. Interested people told other interested people, and soon a gang of a dozen men was following Dantar and Marko as they went in search of lodgings for the night.

When wandering through any unfamiliar city, it is always a good idea to avoid the small, dark streets. The problem was that all of Merk's streets were small and dark, and most of the lighting came from the lamps and candles behind the windows of houses. Dantar and Marko stopped as an idler leaning against a wall under one of the rare street lamps called out to them.

'Ye look as if ye may be lost,' he said, his accent Dravinian.

'Just checking the rooming houses for somewhere clean and without fleas,' replied Marko.

'Third street on the right, lots of nice places there.'

They thanked him and walked on, then turned into the street he had indicated. They had not gone far when they realised that there were no signs or lanterns hanging outside any of the houses. They were halfway along when Marko held up his hand and stopped.

'Not a rooming house to be seen,' he said. 'That clown back there must have meant another street.'

'I've got a bad feeling that he meant this street, all right,' said Dantar. 'There are three or four suspicious looking figures up ahead.'

'There's about twice that number behind,' said Marko after glancing back. 'That's my reward for being trusting.'

'I don't suppose there's a tavern that we could duck into.'

'I think those suspicious looking figures chose this street to close in because there aren't any.'

Dantar noticed that one of the men was carrying a tube with a little flame on the end. He recognised it as a handheld version of the huge flamethrowers on the *Invincible*.

'That's a flamethrower,' said Dantar.

'I know it's a bleeding flamethrower!' said Marko.

'Ah, good, so no explainings, we need,' said someone in clumsy Dravinian.

'Hand over your bag of gold,' said someone else in much better Dravinian.

'We don't have a bag of gold,' said Marko. 'See, only two gold Savarian moonlets and some silver.'

'I'm warning you, this flamethrower squirts a mix of lamp oil and soap. That sticks to your skin as it burns you to death.'

'But all we have is this,' insisted Marko, holding out the coins.

A huge, strong hand seized his and another scooped the coins from his palm.

'Now all of the rest, you are giving,' said a third voice.

'I've told you, that was all we have!' pleaded Marko.

A brief but powerful gust of wind stirred the air of the warm tropical night for a moment. The men glanced to each other in the light from the flamethrower's burning wick, as if winds like that did not happen at this time of year. A towering figure advanced on Marko.

'I'm gonna check your pockets,' he said. 'You just keep your hands up while I – Ouch!'

The man stepped back, clutching a finger.

'Sorry, I've got a trained rat, he bites pickpockets,' said Marko, taking Merikus out and holding him aloft.

'Just flame them both, we'll pick their coins out of the ashes,' said the man nursing his finger.

'Raising pressure,' said the man with the flamethrower, and they heard the squeak of a little lever being pumped.

'You run one way, I'll run the other!' hissed Dantar. 'One of us may escape –'

A brilliant blast of green fire lit up the narrow street, travelling in a neat arc to incinerate all the men surrounding Dantar and Marko. They looked up – and up, and up. Peering down at them by the light of the burning bodies and flamethrower was a fully grown dragon perched on the roof of a house.

An enormous head descended until a pair of pale yellow eyes was level with their faces. The eyes focused on Dantar.

'*You are special*,' sounded in their minds, and in the minds of those nearby.

'Um, ah, thank you, sir,' Dantar replied in a voice somewhere between a squeak and a whisper.

'*The Iron Claw told me that her father has been dabbling in forbidden dark arts.*'

'You've met my sister?' exclaimed Dantar.

'*Ah, your sister, so the rogue warlock is your father. Suddenly I understand.*'

'I don't understand,' said Dantar, but Videnveld was turning to Marko and Merikus.

'*Rat, you are special too, another victim of forbidden magic. Were you not innocent, I would flame you so intensely that the very cobblestones beneath your ashes would melt. Ratbearer human, what is your name?*'

'*I – ah, Marko.*'

'*I declare you to be a dragon guard. Stand firm in my place.*'

'You want me to guard a dragon?' asked Marko. 'How do I do that?'

'*Do not disappoint me,*' was Videnveld's reply, then she raised her head again, spread her wings and sprang into the night sky, leaving the roof that had been her perch in ruins.

Dantar and Marko looked at each other.

'This could be a great time to leave quickly and quietly,' said Dantar, but people were already converging from both ends of the street.

'Make way for the captain of the city watch!' cried someone who was ringing a bell.

A special sitting of the magistrate's court was convened, and Dantar and Marko were brought in, chained together. One of the watchmen carried Merikus in a birdcage.

'At or about the hour of the Night Seagull, I was on my patrol when I saw a yellow light in Piebaker Lane,' declared the watch captain.

'It was green,' said Dantar.

'Order!' said the magistrate. 'When I want a response I'll call "respond".'

'As I reached Piebaker Lane, I saw these two sailors surrounded by a dozen corpses and holding a flamethrower. It is my suspicion that they were trying to rob innocent citizens of their hard earned silver, so that they could continue a drinking spree. When the citizens resisted, they burned them to death with a flamethrower.'

'Respond,' said the magistrate. 'You, the tall one.'

'First, neither of us was holding the flamethrower,' said Marko, pointing to the charred wreckage of the weapon on a table in front of the magistrate. 'As you can see, a charred hand is still grasping the pumping lever, and we both have our hands. Secondly, they were trying to rob us, not the other way around.'

'Then what happened?' asked the magistrate. 'How did you defeat a dozen men, one of whom was armed with a flamethrower?'

'A dragon landed on the roof opposite us and flamed the men who had bailed us up. Its breath melted the cobblestones. You can see that the flamethrower is partly melted as well.'

'A dragon?' asked the magistrate. 'Captain, did you see a dragon?'

'No, your honour.'

'Respond,' said the magistrate.

'It flew away before he arrived,' said Dantar.

'How convenient.'

'The roof it was sitting on has partly collapsed!' said Marko.

'Is that true?' asked the magistrate, turning back to the captain.

'Probably woodworm,' said the captain.

'And there was the voice of the dragon in our heads,' said Marko. 'That's how dragons talk, like in your head.'

'I do recall some odd words being shouted in the distance, something about iron claws, dragon guards and other nonsense like that,' said the captain. 'Probably some drunk raving to himself.'

'Well, what about the flamethrower?' exclaimed Marko. 'A flamethrower's flame can't burn hot enough to melt cobblestones. Besides, how could I burn my flamethrower with my own flamethrower?'

'Ah, so you admit that it was your flamethrower,' said the magistrate.

'No, no, I was just explaining –'

'Condemned by your very own words!' said the magistrate, hitting his desk with his little hammer. 'Guilty as charged. Lock these murderers up for the night. We'll hang them tomorrow morning, just as soon as we can make the announcement and sell tickets.'

'What about the rat?' asked the captain.

'Feed it to a cat, it will be an entertaining fight.'

'You can't do that!' squeaked Merikus. 'This is a Dravinian colony, and gladiatorial games are banned in Dravinia.'

'An enchanted rat!' exclaimed the captain.

'Enchanted animals are also banned in Dravinia,' said the magistrate. 'Hang it as well.'

'How do I hang a rat?'

'Hang the birdcage above a pail of water, then

let it drop and the rat will drown.'

Dantar and Marko were led back out into the night, followed by a guardsman carrying Merikus in the cage. A couple of questions to the guards who were escorting them established that they did not speak Savarian, so the youths began to speak more freely to each other.

'Maybe the dragon will come back and rescue us tomorrow,' said Marko.

'It spoke as if it were going away for a while,' said Dantar. 'I think we're on our own, dragon guard.'

'What about your personal dragon?'

'*My* personal dragon?' exclaimed Dantar

'The one who you say keeps saving you, the shapeshifter rat back there in the cage.'

'I'm not his personal dragon!' squeaked Merikus.

'See, he admits that he's a dragon!' said Marko.

'You're sounding like that magistrate,' said Merikus.

'I think we're back in trouble,' said Dantar. 'That big dragon has flown off leaving you in charge, it called you dragon guard – Wait a moment! That thing called you a dragon guard.

What if that means *dragon that guards* rather than *guarder of dragons*?'

'I am *not* a dragon,' said Marko firmly.

'The dragon seemed to think so.'

'Dragons get it wrong sometimes, there's a very large crater in the side of a mountain near Teliz to prove that. Oi, Merikus, are you sure that you're not a dragon?'

'If my breath could melt wire, do you think I'd still be in this stupid cage?' the rat squeaked back.

'Well then, we're all dead,' Dantar concluded.

TO BE CONTINUED in *Trial by Dragons*